D. F. E. Sykes

Ealing and Its Vicinity

in large print

D. F. E. Sykes

Ealing and Its Vicinity

in large print

Reproduction of the original.

1st Edition 2023 | ISBN: 978-3-38730-168-7

Megali Verlag is an imprint of Outlook Verlagsgesellschaft mbH.

Verlag (Publisher): Outlook Verlag GmbH, Zeilweg 44, 60439 Frankfurt, Deutschland
Vertretungsberechtigt (Authorized to represent): E. Roepke, Zeilweg 44, 60439 Frankfurt, Deutschland
Druck (Print): Books on Demand GmbH, In de Tarpen 42, 22848 Norderstedt, Deutschland

EALING AND ITS VICINITY

D F E SYKES

Ealing and its Vicinity

HE purpose of this brochure is not an ambitious one. It does not aspire to rank in antiquarian or topographical interest with the work of Mr. Falkener; its modest claim is to tell briefly and in simple words such facts connected with the parish of Ealing and its neighbourhood as may be reasonably supposed to possess an interest for the ordinary resident and for the stranger whom he invites within his gates. It is intended to be a great deal less than an erudite tome of ancient lore, and a little more than the descriptive prefix usually contained in a local Guide or Handbook.

The village of Ealing lies on the northern and southern sides of the Uxbridge Road, and is distant about seven miles west from where once stood Tyburn Turnpike. The Parish of Ealing is not mentioned in Domesday Book but was probably then comprised within the manor of Fulham. It is within the Hundred of Ossulstone and the County of Middlesex and in the Diocese of London. Its eastern boundaries are, Chiswick, Acton and Twyford; its western, New Brentford, Hanwell, and Greenford; its northern the river Brent, Harrow and Perivale; its southern, the Thames.

Ancient records present many different modes of spelling the name; Yelling, Yealinge, Zellin and the one now in vogue.

3

The significance of the word does not appear, but it may be connected with Zea-ling Bea-meadow. The parish reaches three and a half miles from north to south, and two miles one furlong from east to west, and has an acreage of about 3,800 acres. It is divided for parochial purposes into the Upper or Ealing side, and the Lower or Brentford side, but the ratepayers constitute at present one vestry.

The manor of Ealing has belonged from time immemorial to the See of London, and the custom of copyhold prevails therein, the tenants' holding being evidenced by copy of the Court rolls. The origin of this tenure is very obscure, but it would seem to have originated with the villeins or tenants in villeinage, who composed most of the agricultural population of England for some centuries after the Norman Conquest, through the commutation of base services into specific rents in money or money's worth. The predecessors of our copyholders were mere tenants at the will of the Lord of the manor, but the practice of the Lord's recognising the claims of the near kindred of a deceased tenant to succeed him in his holding gradually ripened into a custom which was ultimately established by a decision of the Judges in Edward IV's time, who held that a tenant by copyhold might have an action of trespass against the Lord for dispossession. From this time copyholders have been in effect freeholders, the difference consisting in the method of alienation, and in

4

some instances in the obligation to sundry fines, and in the method of descent on intestacy.

In the Manor of Ealing the custom of Borough English prevails by virtue of which lands descend to the youngest and not, as generally, to the eldest son, and if the tenant have no issue to the younger brother. The reason of this custom is, says Littleton, that the youngest son is presumed in law to be least able to shift for himself. This is a curious and interesting mark of the difference between feudal or military tenures and copyhold, which were originally agricultural. Tenancies in tail or fee simple fell on intestacy to the eldest son, because the eldest son was presumably best able to render to the feudal lord the military services which were an incident and condition of his tenure. In the Manor of Ealing lands descend on intestacy to the youngest son, and in default of male issue are divisible among the daughters equally. The widow of a copyholder, if a spinster at the time of her marriage, is entitled to dower and the correlative right of tenancy by the curtesy is recognised. One year's quit rent is payable to the Lord on alienation and on heriotable land, three shillings and fourpence in the name of a heriot. The heriot—Dano-Saxon "heregeat," was originally a gift made by a tenant to his Lord of his horse and armour. This gift became first usual then compulsory, and was subsequently commuted for a money charge. In Ealing as in other Manors

5

there are two general courts, held on Easter Monday and in the middle or end of November in each year. The Courts Leet and Court Baron are held at Hammersmith, and the following is the proclamation summoning to the Court:—"All manner of persons that owe suit and service to our Sovereign Lady the Queen, or the Court Leet and Court Baron of Frederick Temple, Lord Bishop of London Lord of the Manor of Ealing, held this day for the said Manor, may give attendance here, and come into court and take their admission." On a conveyance of lands a surrender is made in form following:—

"You do by me, and by this rod, surrender into the hands of the Lord of the Manor of Ealing, all that copyhold messuage, and this surrender you make to the use and behalf of A. B. according to the custom of the Manor."

The history of most manors up to the time at all events of the great development of England as a mercantile power is the history of the lord of the manor. If one turns to almost any of the many histories of particular towns, it will be found that such accounts are in the main those of the fortunes of some noble family. It is inevitable that it should be so. During the early times after the complete introduction of the feudal system into this country, a town or village was a mere appanage of a Lordship. During the wars of Stephen, and in

6

the more disastrous wars of the Roses, Manors were in the hands now of this, now of that, potent Prince or Lord.

Manors changed their lords with the political seasons. Attainders for high treason were of the commonest occurrence, and the Crown seized on forfeited lands and transferred them to new favourites. The caprices of a Court favourite, the humours of a royal mistress, the rivalries of contending houses no less than reasons of State affected the ownership of broad domains, and the faithful recorder of the growth of towns that are now great hives of industry had little to enrich his volumes save the vicissitudes of courts and the fortunes of barons of high degree. But such stories are not to be looked for in the history of Ealing. As we have said the Lordship of Ealing has reposed from time immemorial, such that the memory of man runneth not to the contrary, in the curious terminology of the law, in the Church. When all around was in seething turmoil the Church changed not. But once, in that great upheaval we call the Reformation, were the lands of mother Church much affected by imperial changes. Whether the Normans, Plantagenets, Tudors or Stuarts ruled, the Manors of the Church were, in the main, secure from the hands of sacrilege. When fierce barons were fiercest, when intestine troubles were most rife, lands in the Dead Hand were, as a rule, unmolested. And it is to this continuity of possession, this

7

holding by a Corporation sole that never dies, this sacerdotal character of its Lordship, that Ealing owes its immunity from those storms that have raged round other and less happy fiefs. And its inland position has been again a security. It has not been exposed, as border towns have been exposed, to the raids of restless tribes or hostile neighbours. It is too far removed from the mouth of the river to make it a place of strategic importance, and though it has not escaped the tramp of armed men, it has been the scene of no memorable siege or bloody fray.

Murder Of Edmund Ironside At Brentford.

The neighbouring town of Brentford has a less happy fate, and Ealing doubtless shared to some extent in the events at Brentford. In the year 1016, Ethelred, the King, dying, the country was torn by the rival claims of Edmund Ironside and Canute. London and the parts about it declared for Edmund, the remoter counties ranging themselves with the Danish King. A sharp engagement between the hostile forces gave a temporary victory to Edmund, and the Danes fled across the Thames, many of the Saxons being, in the ardour of the pursuit, drowned in the river near where Kew Bridge now stands. Edmund did not live to reap substantial advantages from this triumph, for not long afterwards he was assassinated at Brentford. The murderer was the son of Edric Strone who had allied himself with Canute. The event is narrated by Henry de Huntingdon: "King Edmund some days after this was killed treacherously at Brentford. Thus he fell while he flourished in his Kingdom, feared and dreaded by his enemies. In the night he went in some house, where the son of Edric the leader, hid in a secret cave by the advice of his father, stabbed the King twice in the belly, and taking flight, left the knife in the viscera. Then Edric came to King Canute and saluted him, saying, 'Hail to thee, sole King,' and made the circumstances known to him. The King answered, 'I am so much beholden to thee for this service, I will set thee higher than any of the English nobility.' Therefore he caused him to be beheaded, and his head to be placed on the highest tower in London."

Battle Of Brentford.

The vicinity of Ealing appears to have known little of the horrors of war, from the time of Canute to that of the Civil war when, on November 12th, 1642, an engagement took place at Brentford between the Royalist and Parliament forces, which though of no great magnitude was the occasion of much recrimination between the King and his disaffected subjects, as it occurred at a time when efforts, more or less sincere, were being made to accommodate the differences between the Throne and the people. Lord Clarendon in his history thus narrates the battle: "So the King marched with his whole army towards Brentford, where were two regiments of their best foot, for so they were accounted, being those who had eminently behaved themselves at Edge-Hill, having barricaded the narrow avenues of the town, and cast up some little breastworks at the most convenient places. Here a Welsh regiment of the King's, which had been faulty at Edge-Hill recovered its honour, and assaulted the works and forced the barricades, well defended by the enemy. Then the King's forces entered the town, after a very warm service; the chief officers, and many soldiers of the other side being killed; and they took there about five hundred prisoners, eleven colours, and fifteen pieces of cannon and good store of ammunition. But this victory, for considering the place, it might well be called so, proved not at all fortunate to his Majesty." An officer of the King's says of his colonel in this battle (Sir Edward Tritton,) that "it was his happy honour (assisted by God and a new piece of cannon newly come up) to drive the Roundheads from their works, where it was an heart breaking object to hear and see the miserable deaths of many goodly men; we slew a Lieutenant Colonel, two Sergeant Majors, some Captains, and other officers and soldiers there, about thirty or forty of them, and took four hundred prisoners. But what was most pitiful was, to see how many poor men ended and lost their lives, striving to save them, for they run into the Thames, and about two hundred of them, as we might judge, were there drowned by themselves, and so were guilty of their own deaths; for had they stayed and yielded up themselves, the King's mercy is so gracious that he had spared them all." The first blood was shed in the civil war at Edgehill, on Sunday, October 23rd, 1642, so that when the encounter took place at Brentford the young officer whose letter survives him, was fresh to the gruesome attendants of war, and it may be presumed that if he had the good luck to see its end, he was less appalled by the sights he witnessed than he seems to have been, after what was probably his baptism of fire at Brentford. However, that affair, trivial as in some aspects it appears, served unhappily to fan the flame, and of course each side was anxious to throw the responsibility for the bloodshed upon the other. Each side was anxious to say "You began it." The Parliamentarians, as we have said, were defeated at Brentford, but they made their defeat a sort of object lesson, as we should call it nowadays, to serve to stimulate their adherents throughout the Kingdom. A commission was appointed to enquire into the alleged barbarities of the King's forces, and their report is so amusing a specimen of special pleading that it deserves to be

11

reproduced. It is noteworthy also that the House of Commons ordered that "The Minister of Middlesex and parts of London, do the next fast-day read in their several parish-churches the account of the sufferings of the inhabitants of Old Brentford, on the 12th and 13th of the month by his Majesties forces; and that they do exhort the people to a compassionate consideration of them." "Compassionate consideration" is good and we may surmise that "Remember Brentford" was used in those days much as the historic phrase "Remember Mitchels-town" was used in our own. The report was as follows: "A true and perfect relation of the barbarous and cruel passages of the King's army at Old Brainford, near London, being presented to the House of Commons by a Committee of the same house, who was sent thither on purpose to examine the bulk of the particular actions of the said Army." "The King's army upon Saturday, the 12th of November instant, (after his Majesty's assent to the Treaty of Accommodation,) surprised Colonel Holles, his regiment, at Old Brainford, and after they had possessed themselves of the town, they plundered it without any respect of persons, except the home of one Brent, a Church papist (whose wife was a known popish accusant, and he suspected to give intelligence, to the King's Army.) First they drank and wasted the beer and wines at the several inns, and other places in the towns, and such beer and wine as they could not drink, they let it down out in some cellars as deep as the middle. They also took from the inhabitants their money, linen, woollen, bedding, wearing apparel, horses, cows, wine, hens, &c., and all manner of victuals; also pewter, brass, iron pots, and kettles, and all manner of grocery, chandlery and apothecary ware, nay, such was their barbarous carriage, that many of the feather beds which they could not bear away they did cut the tales of them in pieces, and scattered the feathers about in the fields and streets; they did also cut the cords of the beds, and broke down the bedsteads; they did cut to pieces and burn the poor fishermens' boats and nets by which they got their living, having pillaged them besides of all they ever had; they did cast beef into the dirt, which they carried not away with them; they littered their horses with wheat-sheaves; they spoiled nurseries of fruit trees of good value, and near upon three bushels of apples from one man they took away, spoiled and trampled to dirt with their horses' feet, besides fifteen pair of sheets, his bedding, &c. They also took candles to the value of twenty pounds and upwards from one man, and burnt them all night through the army, and such as they carried not away, either they broke in pieces, or threw into the fire, or trod in the mire. Had they rested with robbing of the richer sort it had been some degree of mercy, but they left not unplundered the blind beggar at Old Brainford, taking from him and his wife their wearing apparel, linen, woollen and bedding; and the like they did to the poor almswomen in the Spittle there, and cook from them their wheel or rocks by which they got something towards a livelihood; and when they had thus plundered and taken away all the goods, except here and there a bed, they defaced some houses and set one of them on fire on purpose, as is conceived, to fire the town, which was afterwards quenched by an inhabitant. Had their wicked carriages here ended in the loss of the inhabitants' goods without hazard of their persons, they had undergone it with more patience, but such was their inhuman behaviour, that they did set drawn swords and pistols cocked to men's and women's breasts, threatening them with death if they brought not out all their money, and threatening others to cut off their noses and pull out their eyes, calling them Parliament dogs, round-headed rogues, beating and wounding some of them, (one of them being a lame cripple,) taking of the inhabitants prisoners, and putting irons upon them, others they tied with ropes, and stripped some to their shirts, and as one of them who was led next day in irons towards Oatlands, stopped to take a little water in his hat to drink, they beat him and bruised him for offering to do it. Their hearts were so scared they would not extend compassion to the aged and greyheaded; for they took one grave old gentleman, above four score years of age, and put him with other of the inhabitants of the town, into the pound, where they were divers hours, and afterwards were removed into a slaughter-house, where they lay all night, it being a most nasty and noisome place; and the old gentleman being bound hand and foot together all night. They also plundered an ancient gentlewoman of about three score and ten years of age, whose age and weakness would not permit her to go to Church for these seven years last past, they took from her all her bedding, linen, pewter, &c., and even her mantle from her back, leaving her in a poor and miserable condition. Their plundering was so universal, that even divers of the richer as well as the mean sort were, and to this day are, inforced to live on the charity of the Earl of Essex and his soldiers, the Cavaliers leaving scarce a piece of bread or meat in all the town. It would pierce a heart of flint to see the tears dropping from the old men's eyes, in expressing their sad condition; and a great addition to these cruelties was the barbarous, merciless, and unheard of usage of the Parliament soldiers by the Cavaliers; for they did put them into a pound and there tied and pinioned them together, where they so stood for many hours, some of them stripped to their shirts, others to their breeches, most without stockings or shoes, and in that condition removed to the slaughter-house, where they lay all night, and next day were dragged away over Houndslow Heath towards Oatlands, divers of them bare foot and bare leg over fur and thistles till their feet and legs did bleed, and were sorely galled. But these may be accounted acts of grace and favor in

15

comparison to what they did to others of them; for when divers of Master Holles, his soldiers, fled into the Thames for safeguard of their lives, they shot at them as they were swimming, and divers of them were drowned."

"They took, after the fight ended, five of the Earl of Essex his soldiers, and tied by the hands with ropes, inforced them into the river Thames, who standing in the water to their necks, casting their eyes on their enemies in hopes of mercy; but, such was the merciless condition of their adversaries, that a trooper ran in the water after them, and forced them to fall into the depth of the water, crying to them in a jeering manner, swim for your lives, when it was past all possibility to escape. Here had their barbarous carriage begun and ended in the heat of blood and revenge, had a little qualified their offence; but so full of inhumanity was their hearts, even before the fight at Old Drainford, with Colonel Holles, his regiment, that they placed ten of the Earl of Essex his soldiers, whom they had formerly taken prisoners at Kingston, pinioned in the front of their men to be as a breastwork to receive the bullets that came from Colonel Holles, his regiment, that the Cavaliers might escape them; but such was the providence of God, that not one of them was hurt, though shot in the clothes in many places, and one of the ten escaped, who was formerly a sergeant to a company in Colonel Essex, his regiment, and in the presence

16

of divers witnesses averred the truth of this particular. And now since it appears by the prodigious acts of rapine, devastation, and tyranny, that these men delight in cruelty, and fight against their own associates, and spoil those that favour their own cause with those that oppose it, what remains but that they be taken not for such as endeavour the defence of the King, but the ruin of the Kingdom, and not as enemies of some kind of men, but as the common enemies of mankind; and, therefore, mankind should join together against them, as it was said of Ishmael, 'His hand shall be against every man, and every man's hand against him.'"

To this precious and characteristic document which was ordered by Parliament to be published, the King's advisers thought it necessary to reply at length, and to that reply Parliament replied, and so for a time rebutter and surrebutter were shuttlecocked between the parties in a dispute which must end in the awful issue of civil war.

Patrick Ruthen, Earl of Forth, in Scotland, was, for his services in this action, created by Charles I, Earl of Brentford, a title which became extinct with him in 1651. In 1689 the title was revived by King William, who gave it to Duke Schomberg; Schomberg's son, who died in 1719, was the last Earl of Brentford.

We have mentioned two events so far removed in time as the reigns of Edmund and Charles I, and they are the only ones in which Ealing and its vicinity seem to have been perturbed by armed forces, but it should be added that when England was threatened with invasion by Napoleon in 1797, the inhabitants of Ealing and Brentford formed a volunteer corps of some two hundred strong, and at the close of the war its colours were, happily unstained, deposited in the Parish Church at Ealing.

The Brentford Martyrs.

But this locality is associated in history not only with war's alarms, but with religious and political divisions. From Falkener's History of Brentford, we learn that "Not long after the death of seven godly martyrs that suffered in Smithfield were six other faithful witnesses of the Lord's true Testament, martyred at Brainford, the 14th day of July, 1558, which said six were of that Company, that were apprehended in a close, hard by Islington, and sent to prison. Whose names hereafter follow: Robert Miles, Stephen Cotton, Robert Dynes, Stephen Wright, John Slade, William Pikes. The six forenamed martyrs (gentle reader) had their articles ministered to them by Thomas Darbyshire, Bonner's

Chancellor, at sundry times, when though they were severally examined, yet had they all one manner of articles ministered unto them, and they had made answer unto the same, in the end the Chancellor commanded them to appear before him again, the 11th day of July, after in the said place at St. Paul's. When they came he required of them, whether they would turn their opinions to the mother holy church, and, if not that, then whether there were any excuse to the contrary, but that he might proceed with the sentence of excommunication. Whereunto they all answered that they would not go from the truth, nor retreat from the same while they lived. Then he charged them to appear before him again the next day to hear the definitive sentence read against them, according to the ecclesiastical law then in force. At which time he, sitting in judgment, talking with these godly and virtuous men, at last came unto the same place Sir Edward Hastings, and Sir Thomas Cornwall, Knights, two of Queen Mary's officers of her house, and being there they sat down over against the Chancellor, in whose presence the said Chancellor condemned these good poor lambs, and delivered them over to the secular power, who received and carried them to prison immediately, and there kept them in safety to the day of their death. In the meantime, the naughty Chancellor slept not, I warrant you, but that day in which they were condemned, he made certificate into the Lord Chancellor's offices, from whence the next day after was sent a writ to burn them at Brentford aforesaid, which accordingly was accomplished in the same place, the said 12th day of July. Whereunto they being brought, made their laudable prayers unto the Lord Jesus, undressed themselves, went joyfully to the stake, whereunto they were bound, and the fire flaming about them, they yielded their souls, bodies, and lives, into the hands of the omnipotent Lord, for whose cause they did suffer, to whose protection I recommend thee, gentle reader. Amen." Why the martyrdom was at Brentford does not appear, though presumably it owes that unhappy distinction to its status as County town of Middlesex, and there it was that in former days the poll was taken for the election of Knight's of the shire.

Wilkes At Brentford.

Readers of Constitutional history are familiar with the struggle between the House of Commons and the people for the freedom of election, contests identified curiously enough in the last century with the names of Wilkes and in this of Mr. Charles Bradlaugh. In the early part of the century Brentford was the scene of much rioting and disorder and even bloodshed, and the route from Charing Cross to Brentford was often lined with eager partisans cheering or hooting the freeholders as they made their way to record their votes for or against the man whom the irony of fate had made the champion of the national liberties.

The Plague.

But if Ealing has seen but little of the horrors of war it has groaned under a visitation more terrible still, the hideous hand of the Plague of 1665 and 1666. It is said to have been brought to the neighbourhood by two soldiers who were quartered at the Half-way House at Old Brentford, and the Parish Register bears sad testimony to its ravages. It raged for more than twelve months, and claimed for its own more than two hundred and fifty victims.

June 24. —A souldier dyed at the Half-way House at Old Brentford, at Don's.

July 1. —A souldier that dyed at James Garraway's.

July 10. —John White and a son of Richard were buried of the plague, from Don's.

July 12.	—Richard Don the master of the house.
July 13.	—Two children of Richard Don, a maid, and a maid of James Garraway's, all buried in one grave, in Old Brentford field, of the plague.
„ 22.	—Sarah, a child of James Garraway's, died of the plague.
„ 26.	—One that dyed in the Burrow at Old Brentford of the plague.
„	One that wrought at Robert Monday's of the plague.
„	The wife of Joseph Grant of the plague.
„ 31.	—A child of Ben Watts of the plague.
Aug. 23.	—Annie, wife of Robert Rendell, of the plague.
„ 24.	—A girl buried of the plague, from Walter's House in the town.

„ 26. —Three children from Brentford of the plague.

„ 27. —Two from Mr. Walter's house.

„ 28. —Robert Randall.

„   Francis Potter.

„ 29. —A child named John Mason.

„   Goodman Carter's wife.

Nov.
10.   —Robert Cromwell's maid.

„   Barbarietta, the daughter of John Welbro' Gent.

In the months of November and December the plague increased in violence, and as many as seven died in one day. Most of the dead were interred in holes dug in the fields to the south of the village, which to this day are called "Dead Men's Graves."

Ealing is rich in noble buildings dedicated to the service of God. The parish church, St. Mary's, stands on the site of a former structure, which was built in 1729, under Act of Parliament and by the Authority of a "brief," replacing the original church that had begun to sink. The present edifice is of brick, and consists of a nave and chancel, organ chamber, ambulatories and a square tower, designed after the Romanesque style, a corruption of the Doric and Ionic. It is basilican in its internal and external appearance, and a baptisty stands in lieu of the southern transept. The monuments from the walls of the former structure are mostly collected in recesses at the west end. The Church is subject to the jurisdiction of the Bishop of London, in whom is the advowson. Robert De Balmers, Bishop of London, we learn from Falkner, gave the tithes of Ealing, in the reign of Henry I, to augment the salary of an officer in the Church of St. Paul's, called the Master of the Schools. But on the office of Mastership of the Schools merging in that of Chancellor, it is probable that the tithes of Ealing reverted to the Bishop of London, for in 1308 the Church of Ealing was appropriated by Bishop Baldeck to the Chancellor, subject to the payment of £ 10 per annum to the Vicar of Ealing, and to the reading of lectures in divinity, either in his own person, or by a sufficient deputy, on penalty of forfeiting the whole profits of the rectory, a third of which in that case was allotted to a lecturer, a third to the repairs of St. Paul's Cathedral, and a third for the maintenance of the Church. In the taxation of 1327, the Church of Ealing was rated at 25 marks. In the reign of Edward VI the vicarage was valued at £13 6s. 8d. The present value of the living, according to the Clergy List is £800.

Ealing has numbered among its vicars many divines who have been celebrated for their learning, their piety, and their zeal, and it is the merest justice to say that in the attributes that adorned his predecessors, in lofty and stately eloquence, in moving pathos, in chastened declamation, and in all the graces of cultured speech glowing in poetic imagery, Dr. Oliver, the present incumbent, has amply sustained the traditions of his benefice. The following is the list of the Vicars of Ealing:—

Roger de Thorlaston.

1372, April 8.   Robert de Haytfield.   Resigned.

1386, Nov. 12. William Semley.   Ob.

1386, Feb. 11. John Dames.   Ob.

1390, Oct. 25.   David Bagator.   Resig.

1398, Dec. 7.   Nic. Bowne.   „

1399, Oct. 18. Will. Wright.   „

1400, Sep. 15. John Duffield.   „

1407, Dec. 21. Baldwin Bagatour.

1437, Aug. 2.   John Mallony.   „

1443, July 18. Joh. Smith.   „

                Ric. Burton.

1451, Nov. 26. Thos. Curteys, LL.B.

1478, May 28. Will. Tournour, A.M. Ob.

1503, Sep. 15. Thos. Everard.   „

1513, Dec. 9.   Sim. King.   Resig.

1537, Jan. 19. Will. Havard.   Ob.

1566, Feb. I.   Oliver Stoning, S.T.B. „

1571, Nov. 26. Thos. Rycroft.　　　　,,

1582, April 7.　Thos. Knight, A.M.　,,

1591, Nov. 26. Ric. Smart.　　　　Resig.

1602, October.Joh. Bromfield, A.M.　Ob.

1610, Jan. 29.　Edwd. Abbot, A.M.　,,

1615, Jan, 19.　Rec. Tavernor, A.M.　Resig.

1638, Oct. 13.　Rob. Cooper, LL.B.　Ob.

Cooper's lines did not lie in pleasant places. He was ejected by the Puritans, and from this circumstance no less than from his position, we may be sure he had not disguised his Royalist sympathies. It is not known how the erstwhile vicar of Ealing spent his interregnum, whether he had means apart from his calling, or lived on the goodwill of friends, or flitted about as so many of the deprived clergy did from the house of one cavalier to another's, or followed the fallen fortunes of the young king *de jure* at the foreign courts that gave a grudged shelter to the royal exile. During the period of his suspension,marriages assumed the character of a civil contract, and the Registrar acted much as a Registrar acts in our days in civil marriages. Here is a copy of an entry of the publication of intent to marry, 1653. "A publication of an intent of marriage betweene John Holliday, the sonne of Jo. Holliday, waterman, and Sarah Walker, spinster, and daughter of Richard Walker, of Old Brentford, mealman, was published in Yling church three several days, viz., November 6, 13, &c., 1653. By me Joseph Walker Register."

During Cooper's deprivation the pulpit of the Church was occupied by Daniel Carwarthen, and by Thomas Gilbert, the latter of whom was in possession at the Restoration. Just as Cooper had clung to Church and King, so did Gilbert refuse to recognize the new or restored polity. So Gilbert was removed from the Church, and as it happened that Gilbert was the first recusant, he desired to have it recorded on his tomb that he was the proto-martyr to the cause of non-conformity. Robert Cooper was reinstated in his old benefice, but died within a few months thereafter.

1660, January 4. William Beveridge, A.M. of St. John's College. An excellent and a most learned divine. In his twentieth year he wrote a treatise on the Hebrew, Chaldee, Syriac, Arabic, and Samarian tongues. He resigned the Vicarage of Ealing for the rectory of St. Peter's, Cornhill. In 1681 he was made Archdeacon of Colchester with a stall as Prebend in St. Paul's. In 1691 he declined the see of Bath and

Wells from conscientious motives, but subsequently became Bishop of St. Asaph. He died in 1708 and was buried in St. Paul's Cathedral.

1673, April 29.Seth Lamb, A.M.   Resig.

1702, Jan. 26. William Hall, A.M.   Ob.

1719, Feb. 9.   Thomas Mangey, LL.D. prom.

The author of many theological works that attained considerable repute. Dr. Mangey was chaplain to Dr. Robinson, Bishop of London, and prebendary of the Cathedral of Durham. He married the daughter of Archbishop Sharp.

William Hall   Resig.

1754, Sep. 29.John Botham, M.A. Resig.

1773, Dec. 10.Chas. Sturges, M.A.Ob.

The Rev. C. Sturges was Vicar of Ealing during the time Mrs. Trimmer was resident in the Parish and in her Memoirs he is described as in every part of his duty indefatigable, admonishing, persuading in season and out of season, exhorting his flock to walk in the path of duty, or to return to it if they had unhappily strayed. The sick were visited, the ignorant instructed, the distressed relieved, and all watched over with a regard almost paternal. It was in the time of Mr. Sturges that Sunday Schools were introduced into Ealing. The credit of establishing Sunday Schools is generally attributed to Robert Raikes who advocated them in the Gloucester Journal of which he was proprietor and Editor. The idea was communicated to Mr. Raikes by the Rev. Mr. Stock, curate of St. John's, Gloucester. Mr. Stock secured the co-operation of Mr. Raikes and though the Schools inaugurated by the coadjutors were not in fact the first Schools which might properly be termed Sunday Schools, there is no doubt that to the publicity and prominence given to the subject by Raikes, we are indebted for the general and rapid adoption of the institution throughout the land, and Mr. Sturges welcomed and encourage the first Sunday Schools opened in Ealing.

1797, Sep. 21. Colston Carr, LL.B.   Resig.

1822, June 1. Herbert Oakeley.   „

1834, Mar. 19. John Smith, B.D.

Edwd. Wm. Relton, M.A.

W. E. Oliver, LL.D.   Floreat.

Within the Church are many monuments and mural inscriptions, but not all of them are of so general interest as to call for record here. There are however exceptions. On the east end of the north aisle is placed an ancient plate to the memory of Richard Amondesham, merchant of the staple of Calais, with brass figures in the dresses of the fifteenth century. There is an oval tablet to the memory of some members of the family of John Oldmixon, a party writer in the days of Pope and Addison, and who secured the questionable honour of a niche in the Dunciad. A black marble table with gilt letters contains some particulars of the family of Sir Frederick Morton Eden, Bart; a pyramid with arms recalls the memory of Joseph Gulston, of Ealing Grove, five times M.P. for Poole, and one of the South Sea Directors, who died in 1766. A monument of white marble is sacred to the names of John Loving, of Little Ealing, one of the Tellers of the Exchequer in the reign of King Charles the Second, King James the Second, and King William the third. Other monuments there are to Major-General Sir James

Lomond, C.B. and to Sir Frederick Wettherall, G.C.H., and a noble piece of ornamental statuary bears an eloquent inscription to the virtues of Dame Jane Rawlinson, who died in 1713, leaving £ 500 for teaching twenty poor girls of the parish of Ealing. A slab on the floor informs us that Elizabeth wife of John Maynard, Sergeant at Law, was buried here ye 4th day of January, 1664. Sir John Maynard's remains are in the Churchyard. He died at Gunnersbury not long after the Restoration. His name will ever be associated with the prosecution of Strafford and Laud and other State Trials of the period. It is said that when he paid his duties at the Court of William of Orange, the King observed on his great age and asked if he had not survived all the lawyers of his youth ? "Yes, sir; and if your highness had not come over here, I should have survived even the law itself," was the diplomatic and perhaps the true reply. A character of very different type found, in the Churchyard of Ealing, rest. His vault bears the epitaph, "John Horne Tooke, late of Wimbledon, author of the Diversions of Purley, was born June, 1736, and died March 18th, 1812, contented and grateful." Happy the demagogue and agitator who can close his life with such a message to posterity! John Horne Tooke, was born at Westminister, the son of John Horne, a poulterer, the surname Tooke being assumed in regard for a friend, William Tooke, on whose behalf he had resisted an inclosure bill for lands in Purley, near Goistone, in Surrey. Tooke was educated at Westminster and Eton Schools, and St. John's College, Cambridge. He entered the Church in compliance with the wishes of his father, but against his own. That the duties of his sacred office were irksome and uncongenial he has left on record in a letter, in execrable taste, to his friend Wilkes. It was largely owing to the exertions of Tooke that Wilkes was elected for Middlesex in 1768, and he was closely allied with that agitator in the foundation of the society for supporting the Bill of Rights, and in the contests in which that politician engaged with Parliament. Tooke obtained his degree of M.A. though not without opposition, many members of the University resisting the conferment, Dr. Paley among others, and in his political strife Tooke drew upon him the bitter invective of Junius. On the breaking out of the American War of Independence, Tooke sympathized with the revolted colonists, and assualted the ministry so unguardedly that he was tried for libel, fined and imprisoned. On his release he sought to be called to the bar, but the Benchers rejected him as a clergyman. He unsuccessfully contested Westminster on more than one occasion, but in 1801 he was returned by Lord Camelford for the rotten borough of Old Sarum, an anomalous position for an advanced reformer. Tooke was the last clergyman to sit in the Commons, an act being passed in 1802 to disqualify clergymen in holy orders. Tooke's chief claim to fame rests however on his "Diversions of Purley," a sort of Grammatical and Philological Treatise couched in Dialogue. Tooke's was a troubled life. What was the secret of the epitaph?

There are many charities, more noble monuments of the dead then ought ever graved by the sculptor's art. The chief of these are John Bowman's Charity (1612) for such goodly and charitable uses as the officers thereof for the time being shall deem meet and convenient; Richard and Mary Need's, a Brentford Charity; Richard Taylor's and Lady Capell's Bequest, by which one-twelfth part of the income of an estate in Kent, called Perry-court Farm was given in 1721 by the will of the Rt. Hon. Dorothy Dowager Lady Capell, for the support of the Charity School of Ealing, and Dame Jane Rawlinson's Bequest, by her will of October 7th, 1712, which has been already mentioned. Particulars of these and many others may be found in Falkner's History of Ealing.

Fifty years ago there was but one Church in Ealing, there are now eight, besides Chapels; *Christ Church* which was built in 1852 at a cost of £10,000. It is in the Geometrical Decorated style, was designed by Sir Gilbert Scott and is of singular grace and beauty. *St. John's Church* in Ealing Dean was built in 1876 of brick, with stone and terra cotta facings in the Early English style of architecture. *St. Stephen's Church*, near Castle Hill, erected in 1875 is of Gothic Style. There are also the Churches of *St. Matthew's* in the North Common Road, *St. Peter's* in the Mount Park Road, *St. James's* in the Alexandria Road, Ealing Dean, and *St. Saviour's* in Grove Place. There are moreover Presbyterian, Congregational, Baptist and Primitive Methodist Chapels.

Mansions.

As might be expected, Ealing and its vicinity abound in noble mansions, large and stately dwellings, standing in rich and ornate grounds, surrounded by lofty walks, and sheltered by noble trees. Here for generations the great and noble have sought repose from the distractions of society, the studious have found quiet and serenity, the statesman calm, the gallant soldier peace, the merchant prince contentment, and all a sweet and healthful retirement. On Castlebar Hill stood formerly Castle-hill Lodge, which up to the year 1812 was the seat of the Duke of Kent, and at one time the residence of Mrs. Fizherbert. The Duke of Kent married in 1818 a princess of the House of Coburg, and our gracious Queen Victoria was issue of this alliance. At the eastern extremity of Ealing is Fordhook, where Fielding dwelt until he left England for Lisbon in the last desperate search for health. It was at Fordhook that "Tom Jones" and "Amelia" were written. His Journal under date Wednesday, June 16th, 1754, contains the following touching passage.

"On this day, the most melancholy sun I ever beheld arose, and found me awake at my house at Fordhook. By the light of the sun I was, in my own opinion, last to behold, and take leave of some of those creatures on whom I doated with a mother-like fondness, guided by nature and passion, and uncured and unhardened by all the doctrine of that philosophical school, where I had learned to bear pains and despise death. In this situation, as I could not conquer nature, I submitted entirely to her, and she made as great a fool of me as she had ever done of any woman whatsoever; under pretence of giving me leave to enjoy, she drew me on to suffer the company of my little ones during eight hours; and I doubt not, whether in that time I did not undergo more than in all my distemper. At twelve o'clock precisely my coach was at the door, which was no sooner told me than I kissed my children round, and went into it with some little resolution. My wife, who behaved more like a heroine and a philosopher, though at the same time the tenderest mother in the world, and my eldest daughter followed me; some friends went with us, and others here took their leave; and I heard my behaviour applauded with many murmurs and praises, to which I knew I had no title; as all other such philosophers may, if they have any modesty, confess in the like occasion." Fielding died at Lisbon in the following October. Fordhook was subsequently occupied by Lady Byron, the poet's hapless wife, and here, in 1853, their daughter "Ada, sole daughter of my house and heart," was married in the drawing room by special license to the Earl of Lovelace.

But novelists as great if not greater than Fielding have sojourned in Ealing. Thackeray was at school here, of which more anon. Dickens used often to ride over to visit his sister, Mrs. Hogarth, at Ealing Dean. Dibdin wrote many of his best songs at his house in Hanger Lane; and Edward Bulwer Lytton was at school in a house that stood in what was then called Love Lane. The school was kept by Mr. Wallington, and a correspondent of Lytton's biographer furnishes us with an interesting sketch of school and pedagogue.

"We drew up in front of a massive old-fashioned arched door in a high brick wall, above which nothing but the chimneys and projecting gables of the attic windows of Mr. Wallington's house were visible. It was a large, ancient, time-worn edifice, in which the lord of the manor or other great man of the parish, might be supposed to have lived in the time of William and Mary or Queen Anne, but it had been disfigured by a mean-looking brick building tacked to its northern side, possibly by its present proprietor."

"I was not long in discovering that Mr. Wallington was not the scholar I had hoped to find him. Not only had he no objection to our preparing our lesson by the help of English translations, but at lessons he used a like 'crib' and, even with its assistance, failed as often as not, to explain the grammatical structure, or throw light upon the meaning of some passage in Sophodes or Thucydides, which had baffled Gore, by far the most advanced student of our lot. Nevertheless, by being always at his post, in cheerful readiness to take his share in our tasks, he kept us up so well to our work that there was no falling off in our previously acquired knowledge of Latin and Greek."

"In Mr. Wallington, we had always before us the example of one who in principles, as well as manners, was a gentleman in the best sense of the word; courteous in bearing, pleasant in speech, with patience, fine temper, and a tender regard for the feelings of others."

"Mr. Wallington rode 'Bonnie Bess,' formerly a favourite hackney of George III, for whose service she had been specially trained, and, in order to protect him against sudden assaults, had been taught to rear and trample down anyone who put out a hand to seize her bridle whenever she had a rider on her back. The story ran that Queen Charlotte, a lady of frugal mind, had sold her husband's stud as soon as his malady had reached the stage that there was no hope that he would ever mount his horse again."

It was at Ealing too, during his schooldays that the illustrious novelist tasted the bitter sweets of a first love, and his own pen has told the story.

"The country around where my good preceptor resided was rural enough for a place so near the metropolis. A walk of somewhat less than a mile, through lanes that were themselves retired and lonely, led to green sequestered meadows, through which the humble Brent crept along its snake-like way. O God! how palpably, even in hours the least friendly to remembrance, there rises before my eyes, when I close them, that singular dwarfed tree which overshadowed the little stream, throwing its boughs half way to the opposite margin! I wonder if it still survives. I dare not revisit that spot. And there we were wont to meet (poor children that we were!) thinking not of the world we had scarce entered, dreaming not of fate and chance, reasoning not on what was to come, full only of our first born, our ineffable love. Along the quiet road between Ealing and Castlebar, the lodge gates stood (perhaps they are still standing,) which led to the grounds of a villa once occupied by the Duke of Kent. To the right of those gates, as you approached them from the common, was a path. Through two or three fields, as undisturbed and lonely as if they lay in the heart of some solitary land far from any human neighbourhood, this path conducted to the banks of the little rivulet, overshadowed here and there by blosoming shrubs and crooked pollards of fantastic shape. Along that path once sped the happiest steps that ever bore a boy's heart to the object of its first innocent worship."

Lord Lytton does not disclose the name of his youthful and unhappy love. He was then 17 and she was, he informs us, one or two years older then he. This seems to be of course. Let the male reader ransack his own experience and it is odds there looms before his mental vision some angel of twenty whom he assured he should be sixteen in a few months, and that he felt old for his age. Lord Lytton had soon to part from the nymph, who, his Life by his son asserts, was forced into an early and uncongenial marriage. For three years, in obedience to duty, she strove to smother the love which consumed her; and when she sunk under the conflict, and death was about to release her from the obligations of marriage and life itself, she wrote a letter to her youthful adorer and with her dying hand informed him of the suffering which she had passed, and of her unconquerable devotion to him, and intimated a wish that he should visit her grave. It is she whom he apostrophizes in one of his earliest essays: "My lost, my buried, my unforgotten! you, whom I knew in the first fresh years of life, you, who were snatched from me before one leaf of the Summer of Youth and of love was withered; you over whose grave, yet a boy, I wept away half the softness of my soul, now that I know the eternal workings of the world, and the destiny of all human ties, I rejoice that you are no more! that custom never dulled the music of your voice, the pathos and the magic of your sweet eyes, that the halo of a dream was round you to the last! had you survived till now, we should have survived, not our love indeed, but all that renders love most divine," and so the noble writer goes on in an ecstatic passage which means, if it has any meaning at all, that he was glad the lady died, because if she had lived they would have tired of each other.

On rising ground on the outskirts of Ealing where it borders on Turnham Green, stands the historic mansion of Gunnersbury, now owned by Baron Rothschild. The present mansion replaces an earlier edifice, which was pulled down at the end of the last century. The Gunnersbury of that date vied with Holland House and Strawberry Hill. At one time the old building was the abode of Sergeant Maynard who died there in 1690. There for many years dwelt his widow, his third wife, who ultimately married the Earl of Suffolk. On her death in 1721 Gunnersbury was acquired by Lord Hobart and later by the Princess Amelia, daughter of George II, and aunt of George III, who formed a Salon there. The princess had a considerable taste and talent for political intrigue, and her parties were resorted to by all that sought favor at Court. In 1761 we find in a letter of Sir Horace Walpole, "I was sent for again to dine at Gunnersbury on Friday, and was forced to send to town for a dress coat and a sword. There were the Prince of Wales, the Prince of Mecklenburgh, the Duke of Portland, Lord Clanbrassil, Lord and Lady Clermont, Lord and Lady Southampton, Lord Pelham and Mrs. Howe. The Prince of Mecklenburgh was back to Windsor after coffee, and the Prince and Lord and Lady Clermont to town after tea, to hear some new French plays at Lady William Gordon's. The Princess, Lady Barrymore, and the rest of us played three games at commerce till ten. I am afraid that I was tired, and gaped. While we were at the Dairy, the Princess insisted on my making some verses on Gunnersbury, I pleaded superannuation, but she would not excuse me." The mansion, the present seat of Baron Rothschild, is surrounded by grounds of considerable extent and laid out with much care and taste. The house contains many noticeable statues, and several striking pictures, one of which limns a historic scene, the introduction of the late Baron Lionel Rothschild into the House of Commons in 1858 after the removal of the Disabilities of the Jews. The baron's sponsors were Lord John Russel and Bernal Osborne, of witty memory, and on the front benches on either side are to be seen the well-known faces of Lord Palmerstone, Mr. Disraeli, Mr. Gladstone, Cornewall Lewis, and the late Lord Derby.

42

Gunnersbury House, says Mr. Falkner, is a handsome specimen of the Tuscan order. The South front is 126 feet long, and consists of a centre and wings; the former is three stories high, and the latter two stories. The north front is of the same dimensions, but of more simple construction; it is ornamented with a grand portico with four columns of the Tuscan order; the whole front consisting of three stories. The east end is 60 feet wide, and is divided into two large and splendid bow windows, and is used as a conservatory. The terrace in front of the house is bordered by a dwarf wall and stone coping, and ornamented with vases. At the east end of this terrace is an alcove, in which is placed a statue of Apollo. The west end is bounded by an architectural archway, leading to the gardens. On the west is a handsome temple of the Tuscan order, supported by two pilasters and two columns. On the tympanum of the pediment is a shield with foliage. The interior is chastely arranged, and beautifully furnished with Chinese vases, antique chairs, &c., and the walls are ornamented with bas reliefs, representing the most striking scenes taken from the history of Greece. From the south front of this temple is obtained an extensive view of the surrounding country including Kew Gardens, and the Surrey Hills in the distance. This spot is the most elevated part of the grounds, as well as the most beautiful, and is further ornamented with a circular piece of water, consisting of about two acres. This part of the garden shows evident marks of the hand of Kent, who was employed by Mr. Turner for the purpose of embellishing the grounds and improving the landscape. A row of cedar trees here raise their majestic heads, and are greatly admired. The Italian garden at the back of the Temple is embellished with eight figures on sand-stone of Burns's "Jolly Beggars," admirably executed by Thoms.

On the edge of Ealing Common stands The Grove, which, in the later part of the seventeenth century, was occupied by Sir William Trumbull, the friend of Pope, and Secretary of State to William III. Pope wrote his epitaph:

> A pleasing form, a firm, yet cautious mind;
>
> Sincere, though prudent; constant, yet resign'd,
>
> Honour unchang'd, a principle profest,
>
> Fix'd to one side, but mod'rate to the rest,
>
> An honest courtier, yet a patriot too;
>
> Just to his prince, and to his country true;
>
> Fill'd with the sense of age, the fire of youth,
>
> A scorn of wrangling, yet a zeal for truth.
>
> A gen'rous faith, from superstition free,

A love to peace, and hate of tyranny;

Such this man was, who now, from earth remov'd,

At length enjoys the liberty he lov'd.

Elm Grove passed successively into the hands of Dr. Hedges, secretary to Queen Anne, and Dr. Egerton, Bishop of Durham, and Lord Kinnair from the heirs of which nobleman it was purchased by the Rt. Hon. Spencer Percival, Chancellor of the Exchequer, who was shot on May 11th, 1812, as he was entering the lobby of the House of Commons, by one Bellingham, whose mind had been unhinged by commercial misfortunes, and who in some way connected the Chancellor with his adversities. Bellingham was hanged at Newgate. Elm Grove became subsequently an Asylum for the officers of the East Indian Company, and was purchased by Baron Rothschild, and is now dismantled.

The crime and execution of Bellingham recall another event connected with Ealing the story of which is infinitely sad. It is a story of great talents prostituted to base uses, with dismal tragedy in their train. In the year 1766 the Manor House, subsequently called Goodenough House, was occupied by Dr. Dodd as a boarding School for young gentlemen, and in February of that year, he was there arrested and conveyed to Newgate on a charge of forging the name of Lord Chesterfield to a receipt for money and a bond. The prisoner acknowledged his guilt and alleged the stress of poverty. The jury returned a verdict of guilty, but drew up a recommendation to His Majesty for mercy. The sheriff of London, attended by the City Remembrancer, presented a memorial from the city to the King, entreating mercy; another was sent to the Queen from the Magdalen Hospital, in whose institution Dr. Dodd had borne an active part. Lord Percy handed in one signed by twenty thousand inhabitants of Westminster, and the wife of the unhappy man with whom he had lived in the most perfect conjugal felicity, presented a petition for the Royal clemency to the Queen in person. But their efforts were fruitless, and he was hanged on June 28th, displaying great fortitude. The unhappy man was LL.D. of Cambridge, a clerk in holy orders, and a prebend of Brecon, one time tutor to the celebrated Earl of Chesterfield, and vicar of Wantage in Buckinghamshire. He was a man of singular attainments, but unhappily of a profuse and extravagant style of life. It was the old story, *alieni appetens, sui profusus*, and the embarrassment occasioned by reckless expenditure led him to an awful doom. Whilst awaiting his end he wrote his "Prison Thoughts," in which he was assisted by Dr. Johnson.

Ealing House in the Park Road, now occupied as Byron House School, belonged to the Bonfoy family in 1691; in 1715 to Sir James Montagu, Baron of the Exchequer, later to General John Hawke and the Earl of Galloway. A further notice of this house will be found in later pages.

Its Schools. Few, if any, places of anything like the same size, contain so many and so excellent Colleges, Academies, Boarding and Day Schools, as Ealing. Many circumstances have conspired to this result. In the first place, the *fons et origo*, probably, of this consummation, nature seems to have marked the spot for schools. The situation is near enough to the Thames to make the loveliest haunts of the river easily accessible, and it is distant enough to be free from the fogs and low humours of a riparian situation; it is remote enough from London to be almost pastoral in its charms yet close enough to be reached by many routes within an hour. The streets of the town and the urban roads are broad and well made, the latter lined with noble chestnuts that, in the spring, are a mass of spiked bloom, suggesting the boulevards of continental cities rather than the prosaic high ways of English life. It abounds in large open spaces, wide stretching greens and commons, everywhere foliage and bloom greet the senses. No noisome factories belch poison into the air. It is *rus in urbe* in effect. The man of business can be wafted almost without effort to the very heart of the business centre of the world, and yet his home lie in gracious avenues lined with stately trees, and far remote from the toil and turmoil of the city and its eternal din. In all Ealing there is not what may be reasonably called a slum, and its most confined and gloomy alley might almost claim to rank as an open space compared with the crowded courts of the East End. Little wonder that the schoolmaster who is often spoken of as abroad is very much at home in Ealing. The illustrious men, distinguished in every pursuit of life, in arms, in commerce, in the calm of the cloister, and in the strife of the forum, in literature and in arts, who have drunk their first draughts of the Pierian Spring at Ealing, their names are many, illustrious, and historic. The most celebrated Private School in Great Britain, beyond question, was that kept in Ealing by Dr. Nicholas, and known as the Great Ealing School. It stood formerly on the site of the present Post Office in Ranelagh Road, and that of the buildings on the opposite side of the Ranelagh Road now used as a Repository. The House now called Thorne House, or St. Mary's College, conducted by Mr. Fiscn, M.A., was. occupied as a Master's House. Dr. Nicholas himself is spoken of more than once in Thackeray's Papers as "Dr. Tickle-us of Great Ealing School." How few private schools, indeed can any other private school? claim among its alumni such men as Sir Henry Lawrence, Lord Lawrence, Bishop Selwyn, Charles Knight, Sir Henry Rawlinson, William Makepeace

Thackeray, Cardinal Newman, Professor Huxley and W. S. Gilbert. Charles Knight says of his schooldays here, "my school life was a real happiness. My nature bourgeoned under kindness." The present Great Ealing School stands on the opposite side of the road to the former premises. It was built by Dr. Nicholas for his son, but the early death of that gentleman frustrated that scheme. The School is now conducted by Rev. John Chapman. It stands on a gravel soil, and is surrounded by nearly seven acres of ground, with lawns and orchards. If the list of the conspicuous successes gained in nearly all the Public Examinations of the present day are any augury for the future, the Great Ealing School bids fair to sustain its illustrious traditions. No school could do more.

The former Master's House, we have said, was, with an adjacent row of houses, opened as a school for boys by Mr. Ray. In his hands it became widely known, and was one of the largest private educational establishments in the neighbourhood of London. The present Principal is Mr. Jas. Fison, M.A., (London), who has given regard to the needs of pupils preparing for the Universities, and the Public Examinations. The tendency of modern education is to lay greater stress than formerly on scientific study, and extensive chemical and physical laboratories are now being erected with a well-filled workshop. It is confidently anticipated that these will not only be of service to the pupils at the school, but will be availed of by students residing in the neighbourhood, who seek to obtain practical experience in scientific or technical subjects. A large and well-appointed gymnasium is also in course of erection in the playground attached to the school and classes in physical education will be formed.

In point of numbers the Byron House School, whose principals are Mr. B. Bruce Smith, LL.D., and the Rev. E. J. Hockly, M.A., and which is situate in the Park Road bears the palm. This School had a noble beginning. It was instituted by Lady Byron, the poet's wife, and for many years that lady paid the fees of the boys admitted on her nomination. Her Head-Master was Mr. Charles Nelson Atlee, and in 1848 the increasing years and infirmities of her ladyship, combined no doubt with a desire to mark her gratitude for Mr. Atlee's co-operation for so many years, prompted Lady Byron to hand over the school entirely to Mr. Atlee, and it was carried on by him and his son, Mr. Charles Atlee, A.C.P., till the father's death in 1866, and its efficiency and success may be guaged by the fact that in that period the number of pupils rose from 40 to 100. The school remained in Mr. C.Atlee's hands till 1886, when Dr.Bruce Smith acquired it. It now numbers over 200 pupils, and thirteen resident and three visiting masters constitute a teaching staff of exceptional strength, and their efforts have borne fruit in the University and other competitive Class Lists. One of the greatest living musicians and one of the best of our modern sculptors received their early training at Byron School, and many of the banks and commercial establishments of high repute throughout England and the Colonies have officered their desks from former pupils of the School. In its earlier days Byron House supplemented the Battersea Training College as an Academy for Teachers, and a circumstance of special interest to Masters, may be noted in the fact that the College of Preceptors was practically founded in the private dining-room of Byron House School. It is beyond all dispute that the scheme for testing the efficiency of private schools, which led to the foundation of the Oxford and Cambridge Local Examinations, has done more than any other movement to stimulate education in this country. It annihilated the sluggard school-master, and considerably wakened up the sluggard school-boy.

The Castle Hill School. This School presents one notable feature. Standing in some half-acre of ground, abutting on four acres of play-ground, the building itself has been designed and constructed specially for the use to which it is now devoted. A building whose original purpose is private residence is not always best adapted for a large school, but the architect for the Castle. Hill School with the initial advantage of commodious and appropriate site has produced a School whose adaptation of means to end, strikes the merest observer. The central school-room is 60ft. long, 23ft wide, and 16ft. high, and the sanitary arrangements of the whole structure are beyond criticism. The Castle Hill School was founded, but not on its present site, by the Rev. O. G. D. Perrott, M.A., in 1875, who transferred it in 1885 to the present Head-Master, Mr. E. J. Morgan, 1st B. A., (London) and by him the present school was erected in 1891. Admittedly the Cambridge Local Examinations are a severe test of a school's efficiency and that out of the 19 certificates gained at the Ealing Centre at the last Examination, 11 were secured by pupils of Mr. Morgan, one with first-class honours, speaks highly in the School's favour.

Space forbids the specific mention of all the educational advantages of which Ealing can boast, but lest it should be assumed these are confined to budding geniuses of the sterner sex, we may refer to the Princess Helena College, a High School for Girls, situate in Montpelier Road, of which the following account appeared in the excellent work, "Ealing Illustrated," published in 1893, by Messrs G. Tyer and Co., London.

"At Montpelier Road, we find the public High School for girls, known as the Princess Helena College, which has an interesting history attaching to it. It was originally founded in 1820, as a training school for governesses, and also for the education of the orphans of Military and Naval officers, members of the Civil Service, and Clergymen, having been established as a memorial to H.R.H. Princess Charlotte of Wales. At this time, it was known as the Audit and Orphan Institution, and was situated near Regent's Park, London. Greater accommodation eventually became necessary, however, and a movement was set on foot, under the presidency of Princess Christian, to erect larger and more suitable buildings. The site now occupied was chosen, and the present erection was built at a cost of £10,000, from designs by Mr. S. Bannister, of Lincolns Inn Fields. Although, as we have stated, it is now a Public High School for girls, the original object of its foundation has not been lost sight of, and a portion of its revenue derived from subscription is devoted to the education of girls of the classes before referred to."

Ealing is the home of many charitable institutions and the Training College for Teachers of the Deaf, situate at Elmhurst, Castlebar Hill, under the Presidency of the Archbishop of Canterbury, has a wide reputation. One of the Homes of the London Police Court Mission is to be found in Church Lane, where, under the energetic and sympathetic superintendence of Mr. Robert Marshall, those who have slipped from the straight path, find help and encouragement in the hard and uphill struggle to redeem the past.

The municipal Government of Ealing is vested in a Local Board formed on May 25th, 1863, superseding the old Highway Board with its nine life members. That the Local Board has been enterprising a retrospect of thirty years would amply prove: that its policy has been successful, a few figures abundantly establish. In 1863 the population was about 5,200. It now exceeds 37,000. In 1863 its rateable value was £18,396, it is now over £167,000, That it has jealously insisted that sanitary safeguards should accompany the swift stride of progress may be inferred from the fact that Ealing has but a death-rate of 11:23 per 1000, whilst professed and we may say professional health resorts like Eastbourne, Harrogate, Cheltenham, and Scarborough, range from near 15 to close on 19 per 1000.

For Parliamentary purposes Ealing, with Chiswick and Acton, constitutes the Ealing Division. Lord George Hamilton is the present member, and it may be said that the Conservative view is in much favor in Ealing. There are those who assert a necessary connection between this fact and the abundance and excellence of its educational advantages. This History sayeth not how this may be.

The municipal Hall of the Town Fathers is in the Uxbridge Road, and is an imposing structure in the Early Decorated Style from the designs of Mr. C. Jones, C.E. surveyor to the Local Board to whose skill and care Ealing is much indebted. The Public Buildings comprise a Free Library, Science and Art School and the Victoria Jubilee Hall, largely used for public meetings and popular entertainments. If to this we add that the Lyric Hall furnishes forth a charming theatre, to which the cult of the higher drama attracts the not infrequent visits of world-famed artistes, enough has been said to assure the most confirmed haunter of cities that though Ealing is not Mayfair, one might have a worse fate than to be banished thither. It was interesting in the past, it is beautiful and flourishing in the present, and it has no fears for the future.

CONTENTS

EALING AND ITS VICINITY 3

    MURDER OF EDMUND IRONSIDE AT BRENTFORD. 8

    BATTLE OF BRENTFORD. 9

    THE BRENTFORD MARTYRS. 18

    WILKES AT BRENTFORD. 20

    THE PLAGUE. 21

    MANSIONS. 35